Dear Parent:
Your child's love of reading starts here!

Every child learns to read in a different way and at his or her own speed. Some go back and forth between reading levels and read favorite books again and again. Others read through each level in order. You can help your young reader improve and become more confident by encouraging his or her own interests and abilities. From books your child reads with you to the first books he or she reads alone, there are I Can Read Books for every stage of reading:

SHARED READING
Basic language, word repetition, and whimsical illustrations, ideal for sharing with your emergent reader

BEGINNING READING
Short sentences, familiar words, and simple concepts for children eager to read on their own

READING WITH HELP
Engaging stories, longer sentences, and language play for developing readers

READING ALONE
Complex plots, challenging vocabulary, and high-interest topics for the independent reader

ADVANCED READING
Short paragraphs, chapters, and exciting themes for the perfect bridge to chapter books

I Can Read Books have introduced children to the joy of reading since 1957. Featuring award-winning authors and illustrators and a fabulous cast of beloved characters, I Can Read Books set the standard for beginning readers.

A lifetime of discovery begins with the magical words **"I Can Read!"**

Visit www.icanread.com for information on enriching your child's reading experience.

I Can Read Book® is a trademark of HarperCollins Publishers.

Danny and the Dinosaur and the Girl Next Door

For information address HarperCollins Children's Books, a division of HarperCollins Publishers, 195 Broadway, New York, NY 10007.
www.icanread.com

ISBN 978-0-06-228159-3 (trade bdg.)—ISBN 978-0-06-228158-6 (pbk.)

David Cutting and Rick Farley used Adobe Photoshop to create the digital illustrations for this book.
Typography by Jeff Shake

16 17 18 19 20 SCP 10 9 8 7 6 5 4 3 2 1 ❖ First Edition

The dinosaur was feeling happy.
His best friend, Danny, was coming
to visit him at the museum.

Danny was excited.

But as Danny left the house,

a moving van pulled up next door.

A strange car parked behind the van.

Danny hoped the new family
would be friendly.

A girl Danny's age left the car.

"Hi," she said.

"My name is Betty."

“I’m Danny,” said Danny.

He thought she seemed nice.

“Do you like museums?” he asked.

“I love museums,” said Betty.

Danny smiled.

He wanted her to meet his friend the dinosaur.

“I’ve got a nice surprise for you,”

Danny said.

“Let’s take a walk.”

Danny and Betty walked along.

Down the road came a really big dog.

Betty hurried across the street.

"Uh-oh," said Danny to himself.
"If she's afraid of a big dog,
what will she think of a dinosaur?"

Danny and Betty walked farther.

Near the museum, they met

a police officer on a great big horse.

“Can we pet the horse?” asked Danny.

“Go ahead,” said the police officer.

But Betty wouldn’t even get close.

SEUM

“Uh-oh,” said Danny to himself.
“If Betty’s afraid of a big horse,
what will she think of a dinosaur?”
Danny was worried.
He knew Betty wouldn’t like
his friend the dinosaur.
But it was too late to turn back.

Danny stalled for time.

He showed Betty the hall of cavemen.

He showed her the outer-space hall.

Danny even showed Betty

the hall of people with funny hats.

“Where’s my surprise?” asked Betty.

Danny couldn’t put it off any longer.

“My new friend Betty,” said Danny, “meet my old friend the dinosaur.”
Would Betty run away in fear?
Would she scream?
Danny couldn’t look.

“Hello,” said the dinosaur.

“Pleased to meet you.”

“The pleasure is mine,” said Betty.

Danny sighed a huge sigh.
He was so relieved.

Betty loved the dinosaur's jokes.

She rode on his back as they toured

the rest of the museum.

Betty even got the dinosaur a snack.

When it was time to say good-bye,
Betty gave the dinosaur a huge hug.
"Your old friend is good fun!"
she told Danny.

"I was so worried you wouldn't like
the dinosaur," said Danny,
"since you don't like big animals."

Just then, a cat crossed their path.

Betty sneezed, "Ah-ah-*CHOO*!"

"I love all animals," she said.
"But I'm allergic to furry ones."

Danny smiled.

"Dinosaurs don't have any fur,"

he said.

"They sure don't," said Betty.

"So now I've got two new friends!"